My Calm-Down Books

I CAN MOVE

Caitie McAneney

PowerKiDS press.

PK Beginners

Sometimes I have big feelings.
I get mad or sad.

My heart beats fast.
I can't listen.

Big feelings are hard.
I want to yell or cry.

What can I do?
I can move my body.

I can dance.

I dance to a fun song.

I can run.

I run around my yard.

I can do yoga.
I reach and bend.

I can play a sport.
I kick the ball.

I use a lot of energy.
My body settles.

Moving helped me find peace.
I am calm.

I feel better.
Now I can rest!

Published in 2024 by The Rosen Publishing Group, Inc.
2544 Clinton St, Buffalo, NY 14224

First Edition

Editor: Caitie McAneney
Book Design: Rachel Rising

Photo Credits: Cover, p. 1 Sergey Novikov/Shutterstock.com; p. 3 GagliardiPhotography/Shutterstock.com; p. 5 Olena Chukhil/Shutterstock.com; pp. 7, 11 fizkes/Shutterstock.com; p. 9 Jacob Lund/Shutterstock.com; p. 13 alexei_tm/Shutterstock.com; p. 15 pixfly/Shutterstock.com; p. 17 LightField Studios/Shutterstock.com; p. 19 Gregory Johnston/Shutterstock.com; p. 21 Maryna_Auramchuk/Shutterstock.com; p. 23 RMC42/Shutterstock.com.

Cataloging-in-Publication Data
Names: McAneney, Caitie.
Title: I can move / Caitie McAneney.
Description: New York : Powerkids Press, 2024. | Series: My calm-down books
Identifiers: ISBN 9781642824919 (pbk.) | ISBN 9781642824926 (library bound) | ISBN 9781642824933 (ebook)
Subjects: LCSH: Exercise for children--Juvenile literature. | Physical fitness for children--Juvenile literature.
Classification: LCC GV481.M45 2024 | DDC 613.7'042--dc23

Manufactured in the United States of America